Hey, Where's Perry?

ADAPTED BY JOHN GREEN

BASED ON THE SERIES CREATED BY
DAN POVENMIRE & JEFF "SWAMPY" MARSH

DISNEY PRESS

NEW YORK

LIBRARY OF CONGRESS CATALOG CARD NUMBER ON FILE.
978-1-4231-2781-9
FIRST EDITION
10 9 8 7 6 5 4 3 2 1
PRINTED IN THE UNITED STATES OF AMERICA
G658-7729-4-10227

FOR MORE DISNEY PRESS FUN, VISIT WWW.DISNEYBOOKS.COM
VISIT DISNEYCHANNEL.COM

SUMMER VACATION! THERE'S A WHOLE LOT OF STUFF TO DO BEFORE SCHOOL STARTS, AND *PHINEAS* AND *FERB* PLAN TO DO IT ALL! MAYBE THEY'LL BUILD A ROCKET, OR FIND FRANKENSTEIN'S BRAIN...WHATEVER THEY DO, THEY'RE SURE TO ANNOY THEIR SISTER, *CANDACE*. MEANWHILE, THEIR FAMILY PET, *PERRY* THE PLATYPUS, LEADS A DOUBLE LIFE AS *AGENT P*, FACING OFF AGAINST THE DEVIOUS *DR. DOOFENSHMIRTZ!*

"OH, THERE YOU ARE, PERRY!"

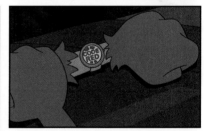

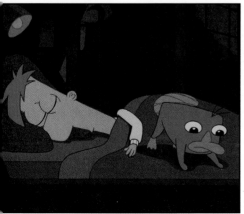

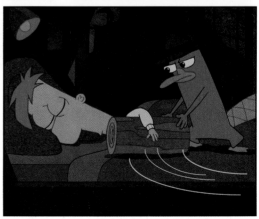

NO MORE PEACH AND PUMPERNICKEL SANDWICHES BEFORE BED.

WHAA--?!

!

YOU!

~CHITTER CHITTER~

FOR AN ANIMAL THAT DOESN'T DO MUCH, YOU SURE KNOW HOW TO MAKE A MESS OF THINGS!

doop da-da

dee-da
doop

doop
da-dee
da

PERRY!

GOOD MORNING, AGENT P. I'VE GOT BAD NEWS AND GOOD NEWS. THE **BAD** NEWS IS, YOU'RE BEING REASSIGNED TO A NEW, **MORE EVIL** VILLAIN.

HIS NAME, **"THE REGURGITATOR."**

WE KEEP PUSHING HIM DOWN, BUT HE KEEPS COMING BACK UP.

THAT'S NOT FUNNY, CARL! IT'S JUST DISGUSTING.

YOU LAUGHED EARLIER.

IT WAS A PITY LAUGH. **ANYWAY,** DOCTOR DOOFENSHMIRTZ HAD TO BE DOWNGRADED TO "MINOR THREAT" STATUS.

WE'VE JUST ASSIGNED **AGENT S** TO HIS CASE.

THE **GOOD** NEWS IS, YOU ARE BEING RELOCATED AWAY FROM YOUR HOST FAMILY TO THIS NEW FAMILY IN THE QUAD-STATE AREA.

PSST! IT'S THE OTHER WAY AROUND, SIR.

OH, OH, YES, YES. OF COURSE. UH, BAD NEWS IS THE RELOCATION AND THE GOOD NEWS IS THE NEW VILLAIN THING.

JUST MAKE SURE YOU TAKE YOUR BELONGINGS FROM THE HOUSE WHEN YOU LEAVE.

THE NEXT DAY...

GOOD MORNING, CANDACE!

WHAT'S SO GREAT ABOUT IT?

NOT MUCH. WE CAN'T FIND PERRY ANYWHERE. HE'S **NEVER** MISSED BREAKFAST, NOT EVEN ONCE.

UH, YOU DON'T THINK HE COULD'VE ARGUED WITH SOMEONE AT SAY, 3:38 A.M., GOTTEN HIS FEELINGS HURT, THEN RUN AWAY, DO YOU?

NAH, HE **NEVER** WOULD'VE GONE OUTSIDE ON PURPOSE.

EVERYBODY KNOWS PLATYPUSES ARE SUPPOSED TO STAY INSIDE AT NIGHT.

WELL, MAYBE HE JUST WANDERED OFF. DOESN'T HE ALWAYS WANDER OFF AT SOME POINT IN THE DAY? AND THEN LATER WHEN HE COMES BACK, YOU SAY "OH, THERE YOU ARE, PERRY!" AND HE SAYS ~:CHITTER, CHITTER:~

YEAH, BUT HE'S ALWAYS HERE IN THE MORNING. I'D BE DEVASTATED IF SOMETHING HAPPENED TO HIM.

PERRY

FWOOSH!

ding, dong!

Doofenshmirtz Evil Inc.

HOLD ON! I'M COMING, I'M COMING!

ANOTHER GIFT BASKET? "WE REGRET TO INFORM YOU THAT DUE TO THE REGURGITATOR'S RECENT EVIL BEHAVIOR, YOU HAVE BEEN DOWNGRADED TO A 'MINOR THREAT.'

IF YOU BELIEVE THIS TO BE A MISTAKE, PLEASE FILL OUT THE INCLUDED APPEAL FORM."

A MINOR THREAT?

REGURGITATOR. WELL, THERE'S A LOT OF *WEIRDOS* OUT THERE.

OH, HERE WE GO. HE HAS HIS OWN BLOG.

WORLD'S MOST EVIL VILLAIN

WORLD'S MOST EVIL VILLAIN?

WHO DOES THIS UPSTART THINK HE IS? IT'S TIME TO SHOW HIM WHO'S *BOSS!*

ALL RIGHT, FERB.

ACTIVATE THE *PLAT-ATTRACTOR 3000.* IF PERRY'S ANYWHERE IN DANVILLE, THIS'LL BRING HIM HOME.

click!

>CHITTER CHITTER<

WOW! I DIDN'T KNOW THERE WERE SO MANY PLATYPUSES IN DANVILLE.

MEANWHILE...

YEESH! WHAT A DUMP!

EH, SO MUCH FOR MR. BIG SHOT SUPER-VILLAIN.

UH, YEAH, HI. I'M LOOKING FOR SOMEONE NAMED MR. THE REGURGITATOR.

DING!

beep!

LAB

VVVV!!!

OH.

DO NOT PUSH

"DO NOT PUSH."

EH.

beep!

YEEEAAAAAOOOOHHHH!!

OW! MY HEINZ HEINIE!

LOOK AT THIS.

ALL THIS TECHNOLOGY AND THEY CAN'T AFFORD A *THROW PILLOW?*

OH, HELLO.

I AM THE REGURGITATOR!

KRAKATHOOM!

WELL. OKAY, MY NAME IS HEINZ DOOFENSHMIRTZ. UH...TA-DA!

YOU'RE THAT DISTURBED LUNATIC FROM DANVILLE.

OH, YOU'VE HEARD OF ME?

YES... *AND YOU'VE HEARD OF ME!*

KRAKATHOOM!

WHERE ARE THOSE LIGHTS COMING FROM, BY THE WAY? WHEN YOU DO THAT-- OH, LOOK!

LOCKED

YOU'VE ALREADY CAPTURED PERRY THE PLATYPUS. MY, YOU *DO* WORK FAST.

WHY DON'T YOU FILL OUT THESE FORMS, AND I'LL CONSIDER YOU FOR A THREE-YEAR INTERNSHIP.

I AM NOT HERE TO APPLY FOR AN INTERNSH--*OOH*, YOU OFFER MATERNITY LEAVE.

YOU CAN START BY MAKING A FRESH POT OF COFFEE!

KRAKATHOOM!

BACK IN THE YARD...

NOPE FERB, NOT PERRY. THIS LITTLE GUY'S EYES ARE TOO CLOSE TOGETHER AND HIS BEAK IS ORANGE. PERRY'S IS MORE OF A TANGERINE.

WHOA, THAT ONE SMELLS LIKE MEATLOAF.

NOPE, TOO FAT.

TOO THIN.

NOPE, TOO BLUE.

TOO ANGULAR.

TOO CARTOONY. HEH.

TOO FRENCH.

THAT ONE'S JUST A DUCK WITH A BEAVER TAIL TAPED ON.

WELL, THAT WAS THE LAST OF 'EM. MAYBE WE NEED TO THINK BIGGER.

AND WITH *MUSIC.* PERRY JUST *LOVES* MUSIC! REMEMBER?

LET'S GET THE GUITARS. I'VE GOT AN IDEA.

WHAT ARE YOU LOOKING AT, PERRY THE PLATYPUS? THIS IS A *GREAT* JOB!

A-AND LOOK AT ALL I'VE ACCOMPLISHED.

I MEAN JUST TODAY I ORGANIZED HIS EVIL INVOICES, SWEPT HIS EVIL LAIR, PICKED UP HIS EVIL DRY CLEANING.

AND LOOK! I EVEN HAD TIME TO DO *THIS!* SEE? "BEST BOSS."

I COULD BE PROMOTED IN JUST THREE MONTHS.

WHERE ARE *YOU* GONNA BE IN THREE MONTHS? HUH? *HUH?*

BEST BOSS

NEVER MIND THE THREE MONTHS. I'LL TAKE CARE OF HIM RIGHT NOW.

WAIT A MINUTE--FIRST OF ALL, HE'S *MY* NEMESIS. A-AND YOU CAN'T GET RID OF HIM NOW! WHERE'S THE FUN IN THAT?

YOU NEED TO EXPLAIN YOUR WHOLE PLAN TO HIM. DON'T YOU HAVE A NEMESIS?

ME?

THE WORLD IS MY NEMESIS!

KRAKATHOOM!

YOUR NEMESIS IS THIS FLOOR, WHICH YOU CAN DEFEAT BY SCRUBBING IT!

ELSEWHERE...

PERRY? PERRY THE PLATYPUS!

HUH? PERRY!

GET OVER HERE. YOU'RE COMING HOME WITH ME SO I DON'T GET IN TROUBLE WITH THE--

YOU HAVE A PET BEAVER?

YOU HAVE A PET PLATYPUS.

TOUCHÉ.

DON'T LOOK AT ME LIKE THAT, PERRY THE PLATYPUS. I KNOW WHAT YOU'RE THINKING.

I'M--I'M NOT SOME LOWLY INTERN. I'M AN EVIL SCIENTIST. I'M *HEINZ DOOFENSHMIRTZ!* AND *HE* SHOULD BE BOWING DOWN TO *ME!*

HEY YOU, MR. REGURGITATOR! LET'S GET THINGS *STRAIGHT!*

I'VE DONE *EVERYTHING* FOR YOU! YOU SEE THOSE HARD-TO-REACH FILES, UP THERE?

WELL, I INVENTED THESE ROCKET SHOES JUST SO YOU CAN REACH THEM.

AND LOOK AT THIS! I EVEN PUT IN THE SELF-DESTRUCT BUTTON THAT YOU FORGOT!

1:37

SELF-DESTRUCT

WHAT? WHY IS IT COUNTING DOWN?

OKAY, WELL, I MIGHT HAVE PRESSED IT BY MISTAKE.

BUT AT LEAST I DIDN'T PRESS THE *RELEASE BUTTON* I INSTALLED INSIDE PERRY THE PLATYPUS'S CAGE.

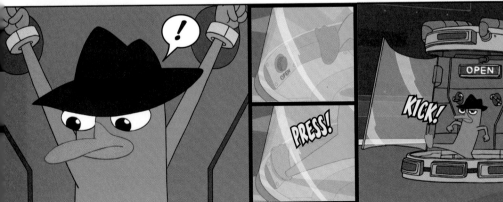

!

PRESS!

OPEN

KICK!

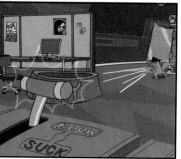

WE DID IT!
WE DID IT!
LOS HICIMOS!
WE DID IT!

FWOOSH

SELF-DESTRUCT

0:04

0:03
ELF-DESTRUCT

BAWOOM!

CONGRATULATIONS, AGENT P, YOU'VE DEFEATED THE REGURGITATOR.

AS A MATTER OF FACT, HE JUST LANDED IN OUR PRISON. YOU CAN RETURN IMMEDIATELY TO YOUR HOST FAMILY.

AND DR. DOOFENSHMIRTZ IS ONCE AGAIN YOUR NEMESIS.

SO IF WE'RE ENEMIES AGAIN, DOES THAT MEAN--

WWAAA!!

CURSE YOU PERRY THE PLATYPUS!

OOF!

OH, NOW SEE, THERE! A THROW PILLOW. YOU GUYS DO IT RIGHT.

BACK TO PHINEAS AND FERB...

EXCELLENT!

FROM THE TOP OF THIS BUILDING, EVERYONE IN THE TRI-STATE AREA SHOULD BE ABLE TO HEAR US.

strum!

♪ PERRY, YOU ARE A BOY'S BEST FRIEND! YOU'RE MORE THAN JUST A PASSING TREND! ♪

♪ YOU'RE LIKE A TREAT FROM A CANDY STORE! ♪

♪ OH-OH, PERRY! WE LOVE YOU MORE THAN ICE-CREAM CAKES! ♪

♪ WE LOVE YOU MORE THAN BUGS AND SNAKES! ♪

♪ WE LOVE YOU MORE THAN ALL THINGS MENTIONED BEFORE! ♪

♪ OH-OH, PERRY! YOU'RE EXTRAORDINARY! ♪

♪ YOU'RE KINDA SHORT AND HAIRY! ♪

♪ THE COLOR OF A BLUEBERRY! ♪

♪ YES, PERRY! SO COME HOME PERRY! ♪

PERRY'S GONE AND IT'S ALL MY FAULT. I CAN'T TAKE IT ANYMORE. I'M GONNA HAVE TO TELL THE BOYS.

HEY, CHECK OUT THOSE KIDS ON THAT BUILDING!

HUH?

♪ SO COME HOME PERRY! ♪

♪ COME HOME PERRY, COME HOME. ♪

HEY, CANDACE. WHY DON'T YOU SING ONE?

UM...

OH, PERRY...

♪ I THINK IT'S KIND OF SCARY... I CAN'T FIND YOU ANYWHERE-Y.... IT FILLS ME WITH DESPAIR-Y? ♪

♪ OH, PERRY... I'M ALLERGIC TO DAIRY... I'M GONNA MOVE TO THE PRAIRIE... AND CHANGE MY NAME TO LARRY. ♪

LARRY?

I RAN OUT OF RHYMES, ALL RIGHT?

♪ SHE'LL CHANGE HER NAME TO LARRY! SO COME HOME PERRY! COME HOME PERRY, COME HOME. ♪

OH, THERE YOU ARE, PERRY.

PERRY!

GOOD JOB, LARRY.

WELCOME HOME.

THE END!

WE GOT *TOTALLY* RIPPED OFF. FERB, LEMME SEE THAT COMIC AGAIN.

OH, FOR CRYING OUT LOUD.

"AMAZING ILLUSION?" "FOOL YOUR FRIENDS?" "DOES NOT ACTUALLY PROVIDE X-RAY VISION."

OH, MAN, THIS IS A RIP-OFF. IT'S JUST LIKE THAT BODYBUILDING COURSE WE GOT LAST SUMMER.

AND I WAS SO LOOKING FORWARD TO LOOKING THROUGH THINGS.

OH MY *GOSH!* AREN'T YOU THE CUTEST THING *EVER!*

AW, YOU'RE SO ADORABLE. I COULD JUST EAT YOU UP. NOT LITERALLY, BUT YOU KNOW WHAT I MEAN.

FERB, I KNOW WHAT WE'RE GONNA DO TODAY!

HEY, WHERE'S PERRY?

AGENT P, DOOFENSHMIRTZ IS UP TO HIS *USUAL* SHENANIGANS, BUT WE HAVE A MORE SERIOUS PROBLEM.

THERE'S A *ROGUE AGENT* ON THE LOOSE, AND HE'S IN YOUR AREA.

CARL IS WORKING WITH OUR FIELD AGENTS TO CREATE A COMPOSITE SKETCH.

FINISHED, SIR.

WHAT? CARL, YOU SAID YOU COULD *DRAW*.

I'M SORRY AGENT P.

IN THE MEANWHILE, HE MAY TRY TO FIND ONE OF YOUR *SECRET PASSAGES* AND INFILTRATE YOUR LAIR WHERE HE CAN HACK INTO OUR MAINFRAME.

SO BE ON THE LOOKOUT FOR ANY *SUSPICIOUS CHARACTERS*.

FWOOMP

FIRST, I'M GONNA NAME YOU MR. CUTIE-PATOOTIE. THEN WE'LL GIVE YOU A COMPLETE MAKEOVER AND TEACH YOU SOME COOL TRICKS.

LOOK, FERB. *THERE'S* PERRY.

MAYBE *THAT'S* WHERE HE DISAPPEARS TO ALL THE TIME.

WELL, IF HE GOT HIMSELF UP THERE, HE CAN GET HIMSELF DOWN.

ANYWAY, WE'VE GOT THE FRAMES AND THE POLYCARBONATE LENS SOLUTION, NOW ALL WE NEED IS SOMETHING THAT *REALLY* IMPROVES EYESIGHT. HEY, *I* KNOW--

--OH, FERB, YOU'RE WAY AHEAD OF ME.

AGENT P, WE HIRED A PROFESSIONAL ARTIST AND GOT MUCH BETTER RESULTS.

WE'VE IDENTIFIED THE ROGUE AGENT AS *DENNIS*.

HE'S A MERCENARY FOR HIRE AND A MASTER OF DISGUISE.

YOU NEED TO STOP HIM AT *ALL* COSTS.

YOU STAY PUT WHILE I FIND YOU A NEW STYLISH OUTFIT.

LET'S SEE WHAT WE'VE GOT HERE.

WHAT AM I DOING WITH A SCEPTER?

HUH, *NEXT.*

FLYNN HOUSE BLUEPRINTS

UH, LET'S *SKIP* THE TIARA.

LEG WARMERS? WHO WEARS LEG WARMERS?

OOH, HERE ARE SOME OF MY DOLL CLOTHES.

~CHITTER CHITTER~

!

MR. CUTIE-PATOOTIE, I FINALLY FOUND--

GET *AWAY FROM HIM!*

I DON'T WANT YOUR *BLANDNESS* TO RUB OFF ON MR. CUTIE-PATOOTIE.

OKAY, WHAT DOES THIS OUTFIT NEED... I KNOW!

I'LL BE RIGHT BACK!

I FOUND IT. THESE SHOES SHOULD COMPLETE THE OUTFIT.

NEFARIOUS? NAH, THAT'S TOO MUCH, EVEN FOR *ME*.

AH, PERRY THE PLATYPUS! HOW UNEXPECTED FOR YOU TO BURST IN ON MY NEFARIOUS--

CUT TO:

...LLIANT EVIL MASTERMIND, HEINZ DOOFENSHMIRTZ, IS WORKING ON A NEW 'INATOR' IN HIS PENTHOUSE LAIR,

DOOFENSHMIRTZ:
Ah! Perry the Pla... How unexpected fo... burst in on my... plans!

(PAUSE A BEAT)

CAGE COMES DOWN. PERRY IS TRAPPED. THE INGENIOUS DOCTOR DOOFENSHMIRTZ APPROACHES PERRY.

PERRY THE PLATYPUS IS DUE ANY SECOND.

HEY, IT'S GETTING A LITTLE LATE. WHERE *IS* HE?

AW, WHO NEEDS HIM? HE NEVER EVEN DOES ANYTHING UNTIL AFTER I TELL HIM MY PLANS.

HE JUST STANDS THERE LIKE A POTTED PLANT.

IN FACT--

AH, *PLANTY THE POTTED PLANT!* HOW UNEXPECTED.

I'D INVITE YOU TO FOIL MY LATEST SCHEME...

SHWIP

...BUT I CAN SEE YOU'RE *ALL TIED UP.*

YOU SEE? I DON'T EVEN NEED PERRY THE PLATYPUS.

LATER...

MOM JUST GOT BACK FROM THE GROCERY STORE SO WE OUGHTA HAVE PLENTY OF *CARROTS* FOR OUR X-RAY GLASSES.

THANK YOU VERY MUCH.

OH, ACTUALLY, CANDACE, WE NEED THOSE.

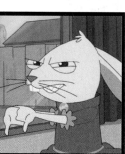

WELL, PLANTY THE POTTED PLANT, SINCE YOU'RE JUST HANGING AROUND, *HAHA,* LET ME DEMONSTRATE THE BRILLIANT *EVILOCITY* OF MY LATEST INVEN--

BARK BARK YIP WOOF

YOU SEE? *THAT'S* WHAT I'M TALKING ABOUT!

EVER SINCE THOSE CONDOS NEXT DOOR STARTED ALLOWING PETS, IT'S BEEN DRIVING ME BONKERS. ALL DAY AND ALL NIGHT WITH THE BARKING, *BARKING, BARKING!*

WOOF BARK YIP YAP BARK

THAT IS WHY I CREATED MY LATEST MASTERPIECE OF EVIL: *THE GIANT DOG-BISCUIT-INATOR!*

NOW I'LL COVER IT WITH AN *IRRESISTIBLE GRAVY!*

THEN IT WILL SOAR THROUGH TOWN AND THE DOGS WILL CHASE IT RIGHT OFF THE EDGE OF THE TRI-STATE AREA. PRETTY CLEVER, HUH?

DON'T GIVE ME THAT LOOK.

PREPARE TO LAUNCH--

BONK!

OW!

HEY, HOW DID YOU DO THAT--

BONK!

OOF!

Doofenshmirtz Evil Inc.

ALL RIGHT, COME OUT IN THE OPEN WHERE I CAN--

BARK WOOF WOOF BARK YIP

BONK! OW! OOF! *BONK!* *BONK!* OW!

THANKS FOR ALL THE CARROTS, ISABELLA.

ONCE THE *CONCENTRATED CARROT EXTRACT* MIXES WITH THE *SUPERHEATED OPTICAL POLYMERS*, WE'LL BE AT THE FINAL STAGE OF MAKING OUR PROTOTYPE X-RAY GLASSES.

NOW I'LL DIP THE FRAMES INTO THE X-RAY VISION SOLUTION.

TA-DA!

OH, NO!

HEY, THAT SOUNDS LIKE IT'S COMING FROM *MY* HOUSE!

MOM! WHAT'S WRONG?

I LOST MY WEDDING RING WHEN I WASHED THE DISHES!

DISHES, HUH?

THIS LOOKS LIKE A JOB FOR *X-RAY VISION GLASSES!*

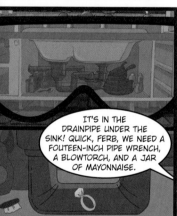

IT'S IN THE DRAINPIPE UNDER THE SINK! QUICK, FERB, WE NEED A FOURTEEN-INCH PIPE WRENCH, A BLOWTORCH, AND A JAR OF MAYONNAISE.

OH! UH, THAT'S VERY SWEET OF YOU BOYS, BUT I THINK I'LL CALL MY REGULAR PLUMBER. HE'S BONDED.

OKAY, SUIT YOURSELF.

WELL, IT LOOKS LIKE OUR X-RAY VISION GLASSES HAVE PASSED *ALL* THE QUALITY CONTROL TESTS.

IT'S TIME TO ORDER A BIG OL' *TRUCKLOAD* OF CARROTS AND START MASS PRODUCTION!

MR. CUTIE-PATOOTIE! WHERE *ARE* YOU? *MR. CUTIE-PATOOTIE!*

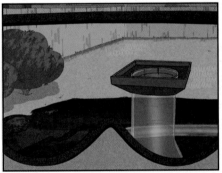

HEH HEH HEH

RRIIIP!

!

UH, HELLO, AGENT--

OH NO! NOT YOU! AGENT P, YOU HAVE TO STOP HIM BEFORE HE--

YES, MA'AM, YOU HEARD ME RIGHT. I NEED *THREE METRIC TONS* OF YOUR HIGHEST GRADE CARROTS DELIVERED *ASAP.*

WHY YES. YES I AM.

HAVE YOU SEEN MR. CUTIE-PATOOTIE? I CAN'T FIND HIM *ANYWHERE.*

WELL, DID YOU CHECK THE BACKYARD? HE MIGHT BE THERE.

HMM. HOW 'BOUT THE KITCHEN?

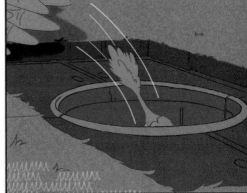

SWITCH!

FWUMP!

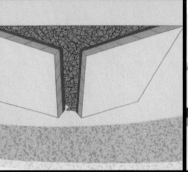

?

chew chew bite swallow gnaw chew chew bite

beep

!

-:GRUMBLE:-

GOOD WORK, AGENT P!

YOU DON'T SUPPOSE HE COULD HAVE RUN AWAY?

DON'T WORRY, I'M SURE HE'LL TURN UP--*HEY*, WHAT HAPPENED TO ALL THE *CARROTS*?

ONE MINUTE THERE'S A BACKYARD *FULL* OF CARROTS.

I TURN AROUND FOR A SECOND AND, *POOF*, NOW THEY'RE GONE!

WELCOME TO *MY* WORLD.

WOW. THAT MUST BE *REALLY* ANNOYING.

OH, THERE YOU ARE, PERRY. AT LEAST YOU'RE STILL AROUND.

DO YOU LIKE WEARING *PINK*?

-:CHITTER CHITTER:-

ON BEHALF OF THE ENTIRE AGENCY, I'D LIKE TO THANK YOU FOR YOUR *VALIANT SERVICE* IN ONE OF OUR DARKEST HOURS.

PLANTY THE POTTED PLANT, WELCOME TO THE AGENCY.

THE END!